School Purchase.

ANTELOPE

GW00728109

For Em and Jack

HAMISH HAMILTON LTD

Published by the Penguin Group
27 Wrights Lane, London w8 5tz, England
Viking Penguin Inc., 375 Hudson Street, New York, New York 10014, USA
Penguin Books Australia Ltd, Ringwood, Victoria, Australia
Penguin Books (Canada) Ltd, 2801 John Street, Markham, Ontario, Canada l3r 1b4
Penguin Books (NZ) Ltd, 182–190 Wairau Road, Auckland 10, New Zealand

Penguin Books Ltd, Registered Offices: Harmondsworth, Middlesex, England

First published in Great Britain by Hamish Hamilton Ltd 1990

Text copyright © 1990 by Chris Powling
Illustrations copyright © 1990 by Maureen Bradley

A CIP catalogue record for this book is available from the British Library

ISBN 0-241-12974-5

Filmset in Baskerville by
Rowland Phototypesetting (London) Ltd
Reproduced, printed and bound in Great Britain by
BPCC Hazell Books Ltd
Member of BPCC Ltd
Aylesbury, Bucks, England

Chapter 1

LAST SPRING, my gran went scatty in the head.

Even after she came out of hospital she couldn't manage on her own. That's why she came to live at our house for a while. I moved into the middle bedroom with my big brother Micky and the back bedroom, which used to be mine, was cleared out to take Gran's favourite bits and pieces of furniture.

"Sorry about this, Tina," Mum apologised. "But maybe it won't be for long."

1

"You mean Gran will get better soon?"

"Probably."

That 'probably' worried me. So did Mum's brisk tone of voice as if she were forcing herself to be cheerful. How could we be cheerful when dear old Gran – who made me giggle every time I went to see her – seemed to have gone a different kind of 'funny'?

Anyway, that's all Mum would tell me. She was too busy thinking up ways to make Gran feel at home, I suppose – such as putting Grandpa Mick's picture on her bedside table and hanging a big WELCOME, GRAN poster over our front gate. Most important of all, she had to make sure there was a space at the kerb for ELF 61.

ELF 61?

Granny's car, yes. If that's what it was. To me it looked more like a couple of tin boxes fitted with wheels and windows but Gran had been driving it ever since I could remember.

"It suits her," Mum always said.

It did, too. Somehow ELF 61 was old-fashioned and kid-like both at the same time so you could never be sure what it would do next. No wonder Gran was so fond of it.

3

She wasn't the only one. Dad and Micky thought ELF 61 was wonderful. They didn't mind a bit that it meant parking our brand-new Honda further down the street.

"Just look at the condition it's in," Dad whistled. "Absolutely tip-top. Could do with a bit of a clean, admittedly, but there's not a speck of rust anywhere. And the engine ticks over sweet as a nut."

"How old is it, Dad?" Micky asked.

"Work it out, son – an Austin 7 vintage 1938?"

"Over fifty years?"

"Bulls-eye!"

"That's older than you are, Dad!"

"Better nick than me, too," Dad grinned. "No beer-belly for a start. And I bet its joints don't creak something chronic in the morning like mine do.

We'll have to find a garage for this little beauty. Needs the sort of pampering Gran always gave it."

"Is it worth a lot of money, then?"

"To a collector, Micky."

"Really?"

"Wouldn't be surprised. Can't be many on the road like this. How about a quick run round the block while your mum's fixing up Gran indoors? You'll see her soon, I promise. We might as well give ELF 61 a bit of a welcome."

"Great!" Micky exclaimed.

Straightaway, he bundled me aside . . . having forgotten an Austin 7 only has two doors. This meant he had to sit in the back instead of being up in front next to Dad.

"Serve you right," I said, sticking out my tongue.

"We'll do without the squabbling,

thank you," warned Dad.

I shrugged and ran my eyes over the dashboard and controls. They seemed simpler, more home-made, than the ones we were used to.

"Nothing automatic here," Dad chuckled as we pulled away. "Nothing plastic, either. Take a good sniff, kids. Real leather, that is. Even cheap cars had quality in those days."

"Real noise, too," I said, listening to the engine.

"What?"

"Noise, Dad. It's deafening."

"Sorry?"

"Never mind."

Obviously he had his opinion of the car and I had mine. I hunched down further and further in my seat in case someone saw us. These streets were full of friends of mine, after all. Suppose

I was spotted in this coughing, spluttering, tinny old puddle-jumper? What a show-up!

I needn't have worried. ELF 61 had something else in mind for me. We were turning back into our street when it happened. The handle on my door – the one for winding the window up and down – suddenly jumped in the air.

Yes, *jumped*.

Honestly, I was nowhere near it. It just gave a little leap – PING! – like a frog hopping into a pond, except in this case the pond was my lap.

"Er . . . Dad?" I said, holding it up. "The handle's broken."

"Broken?" He looked at me sharply. "Have a heart, kid. We've only been in the car five minutes. Are you wrecking it already?"

"Wasn't my fault, Dad," I insisted.

He didn't believe me and neither did Micky. I could feel my brother's glare burning into my neck all the way back to our parking spot.

Micky and I watched Dad fiddle and curse for nearly half an hour before he finally mended the handle. "And about time, too," he muttered.

At that exact moment the petrol-cap flipped itself off. It fell on the pavement at my feet with that clatter-ratter-ratter sound that gets faster and faster.

"Wasn't me!" I said at once.

"No?" Dad growled. I could see him silently counting to ten. "Okay, Tina," he nodded. "Let's put it down to another freak accident involving you. Just don't touch anything else, right? You can thank your lucky stars petrol-caps are easy to put back."

Not this one.

It took almost another hour of puffing and banging and under-breath swearing before the cap was on the filling-hole again. By then, Dad had sent Micky and me indoors.

"You're putting me off," he grumbled. "Besides, I don't want the perishing radiator to cave in or the front bumper to collapse."

"Don't look at me, Dad," protested

11

Micky. "It was Tina who did it."

"I didn't."

"Yes, you did!"

"Didn't."

"Did."

"Didn't."

"Did."

"Cut it out!" Dad snapped. "Your granny's settling in, remember? Do you want to get her all upset on her first day with us? Shift yourselves inside pronto before I give you both a clip round the ear."

This was so unfair I'm not surprised Micky got in a huff with me. He stuck his head in one of his comics and refused to talk even.

Glumly, I watched Dad from our front-room window as he squatted by the back wheel twiddling with the petrol-cap.

13

Bit by bit, it grew darker and darker all round him till the lamp-post by our front gate cast a soft, orangey glow round ELF 61. That's why I can't really be sure what happened next. Maybe it was a trick of the light. All I know is that Dad was nowhere near the dashboard so he couldn't possibly have switched on a headlamp by mistake.

A headlamp?

That's right. The one nearest the kerb. It must have been dipped or somehow out of line because it caught me squarely in its beam as it blipped quickly on-and-off. You didn't have to be a genius to work out what it meant. ELF 61 had given me a wink.

Chapter 2

THAT NIGHT I didn't dream at all about ELF 61. This amazed me, considering what had happened.

Instead, I had a full-colour encounter with Grandpa Mick. This was pretty strange too because I'd never met him in real life. He died in the war long before I was born – before Mum was born, actually. I knew it was him because he wore an army uniform and carried a gas-mask exactly like the picture in the wooden frame Granny always kept by her bed. For some reason I was a lot younger in my dream

– not much more than a toddler, really – and held on tight to his hand as we walked through a garden surrounded by pink, feathery, floating-down leaves. Don't ask me what it was supposed to mean. All I can say is Granpa Bill was just the way he sounded in Gran's stories. By the time I sat down at the breakfast table I couldn't work out what I'd dreamed and what I'd been told by Granny.

"You all right?" Dad asked me.

"Fine."

"You look a bit peaky."

"Didn't sleep very well," I said.

Sharing a bedroom with Micky was what I was talking about, but this wasn't how Dad saw it.

"Over-excitement, lass," he told me. "From your gran and her car arriving, I expect. Thought you were a bit cool about it yesterday. All worked up underneath, were you?"

"Must've been, I suppose."

"You'll soon get used to it. Shall I tell you something else you two kids will soon get used to?"

Micky looked up from his cornflakes suspiciously. "What's that, Dad?"

18

"Looking after the beast."

"ELF 61?"

"Right. That's your job this morning – a wash, a brush-up and a bit of nifty polishing before lunch. Perfect job for a Sunday. Do it properly and we'll go for a spin later. Give us all a bit of a break, that will."

"Granny, too?" I asked.

"Not yet, Tina," said Mum. "She hasn't sorted herself out yet – coming here is a big change for her, remember. Things will be better soon enough."

"She won't be scatty any more, you mean?"

"Let's keep our fingers crossed, okay?"

"Okay," I nodded.

To tell the truth, right now ELF 61 bothered me more than Granny did. Suppose it decided to shrug off a

mudguard or chuck away a windscreen
wiper while I was in the middle of
cleaning it? Wouldn't I be bound to get
the blame?

For more than an hour Micky got on with sprucing up the inside while I washed down the outside. Then, working together, we polished the bodywork till it shone so brightly it reflected the pair of us, all dark and bendy, like one of those distorting mirrors in a fairground.

"That's the stuff," said Dad as he inspected what we'd done.

"Hey!" Micky yelped. "It's starting to rain."

"Always does when you've washed a car, son," Dad grinned. "Rule of life, that is. Don't fret, though. It's only a shower. See, it's easing off already. And look at the gleam you've given it – all those beads of water glittering on the metal. Every one's as sparkly as a diamond!"

I'd noticed this, too. It was as if

ELF 61 were dolled up for some grand, ultra-posh outing.

"Blinkin' wasted on a squitty little runabout like a 1938 Austin 7," I muttered. "Not exactly a Rolls Royce, is it?"

Dad was halfway indoors already so he didn't hear this. My brother did, though. He was furious. "Know what you are?" he hissed. "An ignorant, stuck-up little snob. There's nothing wrong with this car."

"No?"

"Not a thing."

"That's what you reckon."

"What do you reckon, then?"

"I'll tell you what's wrong with it, Mr Micky Brainbox," I said airily. "It's alive, that's what."

"Eh?"

"It's alive, okay? ELF 61 is *alive*."

"Alive?"

Micky stared at me as if he expected men in white coats to whisk me away at any moment. "You're cuckoo," he said, shaking his head. "Blinkin' cuckoo. The first cuckoo of Spring that's what you are."

With a snort of disgust that made him sound just like Dad he gathered up the car-cleaning stuff and left me on the pavement.

Now it was my turn to be furious – partly with myself, but mostly with the car.

"Go on, prove it," I snarled. "Do something special to show you're alive."

Fiercely, I kicked one of its front tyres as hard as I could.

ELF 61 didn't move.

All that did move was our cat, Sandy.

As if the kick had woken her up, she slipped out from under our hedge where she'd been sheltering from the shower. Delicately, like a Duchess tossing away some jewellery she can't be bothered with, she stretched each paw in turn and flicked off the wetness. Then, frisking her coat from whiskers-to-tail, she shook the rest of herself dry. More or less anyway. Enough to impress ELF 61.

Enough to impress ELF 61 a lot.

Because the car suddenly turned copycat – yes, exactly that. With a deft, Duchess-like friskiness of glass and metal and chrome-work, it sent every drop of water spinning through the air as if it couldn't bear the touch of them a moment longer. I stepped back hastily as some landed on me.

"Micky?" I croaked.

But big brothers are never there
when you need them. I was alone in the
street. With ELF 61, dry as a bone now,
standing perfectly still at the kerb.

25

Chapter 3

WHO COULD I tell about ELF 61 being alive?

Because I had to tell someone. "Don't let worries fester inside you," Mum and Dad always said. "It's far healthier to get them out in the open."

The trouble was, I knew exactly what their answer would be. "That's really spooky, Tina. Well done! Why not write it all down for Miss Goodwin at school? She *loves* your storytelling. Reckons we should give you every encouragement."

I could hear them saying it already.

Micky, then?

Fat chance. He was already convinced that ELF 61 had sent me a bit divvy. "Shook itself like a cat, Tina? No problem – we'll put a saucer of milk on the kerb for it every night. Be a lot cheaper than petrol!"

He'd never let me forget it.

That left Gran.

Gran, yes.

I mean, Mum had made her comfy yesterday while Dad kept Micky and me out of the way so wasn't it about time I paid a visit? I didn't want Gran to think I was avoiding her on purpose. Besides, Mum herself had said we'd got to keep her interested in life. "What your Gran needs is something to gee her up," Mum reckoned.

ELF 61, for instance? ELF 61 was enough to gee anyone up, I'd have thought. Maybe my news was just the job to help Gran sort out her scattiness. But I'd better be quick if I wanted to fit it in before Sunday dinner.

At the foot of the stairs, I hesitated. From the kitchen came the saucepan-clattering sounds of Dad cooking. And from the front room I heard voices – real voices not the drone of the

television. Micky and Mum were having a talk. About Gran, more than likely. Now was the best chance I'd get.

In a trice I was up the stairs three-at-a-time, round the bannisters, along the landing and inside Gran's room with my back pressed flat against her door.

"Gran?" I whispered.

No answer.

I coughed nervously and looked round. Was this somewhere in *our* house?

I recognised details, of course. The fireplace hadn't changed nor had the carpet. The bay window was the same, too, with its flowery curtains half-pulled across a view of the ancient apple trees in our back garden, heavy with blossom. Otherwise the room was Gran's: her big, brass bedstead, her dark knobbly wardrobe, her dressing

table against the wall cluttered with
Granny-ish bits and bobs. There was a
Granny-like smell in the air as well –
cold and sweet like scent kept in a
fridge. A couple of days ago this room
had been mine. Now I felt like a
burglar.

"Granny," I called again. "It's me."
"Who?"
"Me, Granny."

Her voice seemed as dry and rustly as paper. "Who's me, son? Come closer."

Son? I was wearing jeans, admittedly, and had my hair bobbed, but was her eyesight that bad?

"Here I am, Gran," I said. "It's Tina."

"What?"

"Tina, Gran."

She peered up at me, her face the same white as the pillow. She'd grown smaller and thinner since we'd last had a giggle back at her house. There was barely enough of her now to bring a bump to the bedclothes. Behind huge wire spectacles, her eyes fluttered with bewilderment.

"Telegram?" she said. "Who'd be sending me a telegram at my age? Except the Queen, of course, assuming she can't count. I'm not that old yet."

"Not *telegram*," I said. "Whatever that is. *Tina*, Gran."

"What?"

"Tina."

"Never heard of you."

I blinked and bit my lip. Not that Gran noticed. She just gave a sigh and said, "Where's my Micky? That's what I want to know."

"Downstairs, I think."

"Downstairs? Don't tell me fibs, child. He's long gone, Micky is. Fifty or more years ago. No sense pretending otherwise."

"Oh, *that* Micky. I thought you meant . . . listen, Gran. It'll be dinner soon so I haven't got long. I've come up about ELF 61."

She looked blank. "ELF 61?"

"Your car, yes. Mind you, it's more like GOBLIN 61 if you ask me."

"Good," said Gran. "I like goblins."
And in the wrinkly voice I remembered
from when she used to sing me nursery
rhymes, she piped up, "There are
goblins at the bottom of my garden . . ."

"Gran, stop it. I'm *serious*."

"Cyrus?"

She cocked her head at me, her long
bony nose making her look more than
ever like an old, faded parrot. "That's
American, isn't it? Cyrus is an
American name, right? Is that what
you are? American? No wonder I've
never seen you before."

"But you have seen me. Hundreds of times. I'm Tina, Gran."

"What, another one? Never had so many telegrams in my life."

"Gran, I didn't say that, I said . . ."

"Yes, dearie?"

I tried to smile. "Never mind, Gran. It doesn't matter. It'll sort itself out, I suppose."

"ELF 61?"

I blinked in surprise. Maybe she'd understood after all. "ELF 61, yes. Do you know about it?"

"Know about what, dearie? I know it was my Micky's pride and joy. I couldn't even switch on the engine without being reminded of him. GOBLIN 61 did you call it?"

"Only a joke, Gran."

"A joke, eh? That's good. Enjoy a joke, I do. And I love the way you call

me Gran. So friendly, Americans are.
Er . . . while you're here there is just one
thing, Cyrus. Maybe you could do me a
favour."

"Yes, Gran?"

"Can you drive?"

"Drive?"

She nodded, her tired eyes suddenly
eager. "I mean, they start earlier in
America, don't they?"

"Not at ten years old," I said.

"Ah . . ." murmured Gran. "Ah, yes.
Thought it might be a bit of a shot in
the dark. Never mind. Thanks for
dropping in, Cyrus. I enjoyed our little
chat. Come again when you're next in
England. I might not be so poorly,
then."

"But Gran –"

"Cheeri-bye, dearie."

Already her eyelids were drooping

shut. Staying longer seemed pointless so I bent down to kiss her on the forehead. It felt cold and waxy. By the time I reached the door I could hear the rattly sound of her snoring.

Chapter 4

THAT AFTERNOON ELF 61 was just plain cheeky – if it makes sense to call a car cheeky.

I brought it on myself, I suppose. Why on earth did I offer to go with Dad in the first place? I should have guessed he'd take Gran's car rather than ours. After all, it was his new toy.

"Fancy that ride, love?" he asked Mum after lunch.

"No, thanks. A snooze in front of the fire is what I'm after."

"How about you, Micky?"

"My turn to do the washing-up," Micky groaned.

Without thinking, I said, "I'll come."

"Only to the Garden Centre," Dad warned me. "I want to pick up some plants and a couple of sacks of coal. Honestly, fancy having to get in more coal at this time of the year. Supposed to be Spring, isn't it?"

It was certainly April. Yet another shower was drenching our street as we stepped out of the front door. "Quick, Dad," I said, moving towards our car.

Dad hadn't got in the Honda, though. It was the door of ELF 61 he pushed open for me.

"Why that one?" I said in alarm.

"Why not?" said Dad.

"But it's Gran's!"

"Can't just leave it to rot, Tina. Does it good to give it a run every so often.

38

Don't suppose it's had much exercise, recently."

"Exercise?" I exclaimed. "It's not a horse, Dad!"

Dad smiled wryly as he started the engine. "No, but your gran's always treated it as a kind of pet. According to Mum, anyway. She says Gran even used to talk to it sometimes."

"Talk to it?"

"About family problems. Local gossip. That sort of stuff. Comes from living on your own, I suppose. When we moved away, Gran felt lost for a while. Of course, we went back whenever we could . . . well, mostly we did. It wasn't easy, what with me changing jobs as well. And Micky and you were growing up so fast. But a visit every other Sunday was never enough for Gran, I'm afraid."

"Couldn't she come to see us?"

"She tried to, at first. The trips fizzled out after they built the new motorway and blocked off some of the side streets. Could never get used to the changes, she said. They didn't fit the map in her head anymore. So she reckoned she never went anywhere unless her old pal ELF 61 bullied her into it!"

By now my eyes were as round as ELF 61's steering wheel. "Dad," I said hoarsely.

"Yes."

"When Gran used to talk to ELF 61 ... when she felt lonely, I mean ..."

"Yes?"

"Did ... did ELF 61 ever answer her back?"

"What?"

Dad switched his gaze from the road to my face and back again. "You know, sometimes I worry about you, Tina."

"Just pulling your leg, Dad."

"Were you?"

"'Course I was."

"You'd better be. Don't want you going funny in the head as well as ..." he broke off. "What I mean is, you save that imagination of yours for your stories, Tina. In real life it could get you

41

into trouble."

"Okay, Dad."

"Good."

He grinned at me to show he wasn't really cross, but somehow his heart didn't seem to be in it. This wasn't like Dad at all.

All the way to the Garden Centre I tried to make up my mind. Was the whole thing a hallucination? Was it just being upset about Gran that made me 'see' ELF 61's oddities? That must be it, I told myself. I mean, what else could it be?

"Tina, you wait here in the car," said Dad as we drove into the forecourt. "Saves me locking the thing. Won't be a tick."

He left ELF 61 with its bonnet pointing towards the entrance. Apart from us, the car park was empty.

Maybe the rain was keeping people at home. "Where I should be," I said nervously.

I didn't like being alone with ELF 61 one bit.

A moment later I knew why.

Brmmm ... Brmmm ...

43

How come the engine had started when I hadn't touched a thing? Dumbly, I watched the handbrake release itself, the clutch and accelerator move up and down as if pressed by invisible feet, the gear-stick slip into reverse and the steering-wheel begin to turn. ELF 61 edged itself backwards.

"Where are we going?" I yelped.

Not far as it turned out. The car halted almost at once. Again, the controls shifted. Then it nudged forward . . . another change of controls . . . and it swung back into the space we'd just left.

Click!

ELF 61 was parked again.

But facing in the opposite direction.

I sat there, stunned. Would Dad notice?

At last he appeared in the Garden

Centre entrance, his arms wrapped round a tray of plants. He squinted up at the sky a moment then, dodging the puddles, loped towards us. Us? What did I mean – *us*?

"Open the door," he called out.

I did as I was told, pushing the driver's seat forward. Dad bent to put

the plants in the back. "Thanks," he said. "Just the coal to fetch, now."

Halfway to straightening up, he froze. "Something's different."

"Sorry, Dad?" I said thickly.

He shook his head. "Nothing Tina . . . except I could have sworn . . . no. I can't have done. Forget it. Won't be a mo."

"Okay," I groaned as soon as he was out of sight. "Get it over with."

I knew exactly what to expect.

Brmmm . . . Brmmm . . .

This time the engine note sounded suspiciously like a chuckle. There was something show-offy about the turn around, too. Once more, invisible hands and invisible feet seemed to be working the controls. Once more the car reversed itself with expert neatness.

Click!

We'd returned to the position we'd started from. How could Dad possibly miss it?

He stopped in his tracks the instant he saw us. The sacks of coal sagged under his arms. "Tina . . . ?"

He shook his head in disbelief. He was still shaking it as he dumped the coal behind our seats and got in the car. "Stupid," he said. "Must've eaten too much for dinner. It's giving me a blinkin' brainstorm."

I cleared my throat. "What's the matter, Dad?"

"Only that . . ."

He glanced from the front to the back of the car, twice. "No . . . it doesn't add up."

"What doesn't, Dad?"

"Well . . . you didn't touch anything while I was gone, did you? The car's controls, I mean? Because I could have sworn it turned itself . . . no. No, that's loony."

With an effort he pulled himself together. "Forget it, Tina."

All the way home we said nothing. Dad pulled up at the kerb outside our house and switched off the engine. Then he just sat there, not trying to get out, his hands stiff on the steering-wheel. Still he didn't speak. At last I couldn't bear it any longer. "Dad?" I said.

"Yes?"

"Spit it out."

"Eh?"

"The worry, Dad. Otherwise it'll fester inside you."

This almost made him laugh. Not quite, though. He opened his mouth to say something then shut it again. In front of us, the next batch of rain began to blob on the windscreen. We'd be here all night at this rate.

"Dad," I said gently, "I do realise about Gran, you know."

"What?"

I put my hand on his arm. "Mum talked to Micky before dinner, didn't she? Now it's your turn to tell me. That's why they stayed at home, right? I'm not dim, Dad. I guessed ages ago. Gran's going to die pretty soon, isn't she?"

He stared at me with that look of total astonishment grown-ups always give kids who spot the obvious.

"You've known all along, Tina?"

I nodded. "All along, Dad."

"Well, I'll be jiggered. Micky, too?"

"Micky, too."

"Blow me. There I was . . ."

He broke off and put his arm round me. "She was a grand old lady, Tina," he said. "Did a lot for me and your Mum early on."

"Was?" I said. "*Is*, you mean."

"For a bit," agreed Dad.

After that we had a cuddle. Leaning against Dad's chest, all I could hear was the thump-thump-thumping of his heart in one of my ears and the pitter-patter, pitter-patter of the rain on ELF 61's roof in the other. My thoughts, though, were all about Gran.

Chapter 5

MUM WAS PLEASED with Gran at supper time. "A whole egg," she said. "And some bread and butter. Swallowed the lot like a good 'un."

"Smashing," said Dad.

"Half the time she's just sulking, I'm sure. If she ate regularly maybe she'd snap out of this . . . this muddle of hers."

"You reckon?" said Dad.

Mum shrugged. "You never know. Stranger things have happened. She needs to keep her strength up like everybody else."

"Does she?" Micky asked. "What for?"

This got him one of Mum's glares though I'd been wondering the same thing. "That's quite enough from you, young man," she said crisply. "I've been hearing about your pranks."

"Me?"

"Yes, you. Telling your gran your name is Cyrus, from America . . . very funny, I don't think. She reckoned you even offered to take her out for a drive."

"Me?" said Micky.

"Don't deny it. You'll be making out it was Tina next. Gran can tell the difference between a boy and a girl, you know – though where she thought you were going to take her I can't imagine. The poor old thing was quite excited about it. She said something about ELF 61 and goblins. Fancy filling her head with a nonsense like that, Micky. These days, it's hard enough for her to

cope with what's smack in front of her
nose let alone jokes from you. And don't
you start sticking up for him, Tina. I
can see it's on the tip of your tongue. It
won't get you anywhere so don't waste
your breath!"

Tossing her head, Mum swept into
the kitchen with Gran's plates. Dad
coughed and looked over his glasses at
Micky. "Trying to cheer Gran up were
you, son?"

"No, I wasn't."

"No need to be ashamed of it, lad,
even if your gran did get the wrong end
of the stick. Never mind your mother.
She's bound to be a bit touchy for a
while . . . we must make allowances.
Help each other. Okay?"

"Okay," Micky shrugged.

His expression was half-baffled, half-
scowling. When Mum came back he

was careful not to look at her.

"Let's get cosy," said Dad quickly.

"And watch television," I added.

While I found the remote control,
Dad built up the fire. Soon even Mum
and Micky began to relax. Snuggling
into a corner of the sofa, I did my best
to have a rest from Gran and her old car
with a life of its own.

Some hopes.

The movie that night was called *THE LOVE BUG*. It's about a Volkswagen called Herbie that behaves all the time like a human being. Probably it's very funny. Dad, Mum and Micky certainly seemed to think so – though once or twice I noticed a puzzled frown on Dad's face. For me it was like the nightmare I hadn't had the night before. How on earth could I tell anyone about ELF 61 now? They'd think it was a story I'd copied from the film.

"What's up, Tina?" asked eagle-eyed Mum.

"Nothing."

"Stop wriggling about, then. Got ants in your pants, have you?"

"Need to go to the loo, Mum."

"Well go, then."

"Okay."

I was up the stairs and into the bathroom faster than Herbie in top gear.

But how long could I stay there? After I'd washed my hands, brushed

my hair, cleaned my teeth and flushed the lavatory a couple of times there was nothing more for me to do short of actually having a bath. And that would make them even more suspicious. So I'd better go back downstairs ... with a paperback from my bookshelf to distract me from *THE LOVE BUG*, perhaps. Good idea.

To reach Micky's room – also mine now – I had to pass Gran's, though. That's how I came to hear the sound she was making. Over and over again. It went beep-beep-beep-beep-beep-beep-beep like a car's hooter that's got stuck.

Gran?

Doing car impressions?

Gently, knowing it was the exact opposite of a smart move, I pushed open her door and looked in.

At first she didn't notice me. She was propped up on the pillows, her eyes on the wooden-framed picture of Granpa Mick she held against her knees. "Beep-beep, beep-beep, beep-beep," she went.

I could see what Mum meant. Gran did seem a lot better – or a lot livelier,

58

anyhow. When she saw me her face lit up.

"Cyrus!" she called in her squeaky, gaspy voice. "I've been waiting for you to drop by. I knew you wouldn't let me down. The trip's all fixed, dearie."

"The trip?" I said.

"We were talking about it, remember? But it's got to be kept secret – top secret. One word in the wrong ears and it'll be over before it's begun. First thing tomorrow is our best chance, I reckon. Come in quick and I'll give you the details."

With a sly wink she beckoned me into the room. Of course, only a daft kid would have done what she wanted. A daft kid like me, for instance.

Chapter 6

WAS IT GRAN's trip or ELF 61's trip?

How could I tell?

All I know is that next morning at the crack of dawn there I was in the car with Gran. Or rather, she was in the car with me because I was the one in the driving seat. Me, yes. A ten-year-old kid. My hands were on the steering-wheel and my feet on the pedals as if I'd passed my test years ago. I couldn't believe it was actually happening.

It was, though.

Couldn't I feel the seat-belt across my chest? And hear the clunk-click of

Granny's seat-belt as she settled in the passenger seat next to me?

"Cyrus?" she said.

"Yes?"

"Mind if we wait here a sec'?"

"Please yourself, Granny," I said.

After all, did I have any choice?

Not that I blamed Gran for needing a breather. It hadn't been easy creeping downstairs in the dark, step-by-tottery-step, with our topcoats buttoned over our dressing gowns. But she'd been quite right about everyone else in the house sleeping soundly. Even Sandy didn't stir when I almost tripped over her on the front door mat.

Now what, though?

Or did I mean now *where*?

Beside me, Gran seemed to be steadying herself. Her lips trembled and her bony fists clenched and

unclenched in her lap.

"Okay," she said at last. "Hit the road, kid."

"What?"

"Hit the road," she repeated. "Isn't that what you say in America?"

"Gran, I don't know what to do next," I protested.

This was the exact truth. I had no idea how you started a car as old as this one. Does it need an ignition key? If so, I hadn't got it. Do you press a button on the dashboard? Very likely . . . but I hadn't a clue where it was. Also, before you did either of these, wasn't there something under the bonnet you had to switch on to get the petrol dripping through?

"Okay, car," I said recklessly. "If it's a ride you're after you'll have to start yourself."

Straightaway, ELF 61 spluttered into life. The pedals moved under my feet, the long, spindly stick beside me clicked into gear and the steering-wheel swivelled through my fingers. I wish I could say I was surprised, but a part of me had been expecting this all along. It was like one of those pianos that play themselves I'd once seen outside a pub – ghost-pianos, Micky calls them. Was this a ghost-car, then? Were we ghost-passengers?

"Beep-beep, beep-beep," Gran sang out.

"Beep-beep, beep-beep," answered ELF 61.

I shook my head helplessly. "This

can't be true," I wailed. "It's all a dream, really – it's got to be."

Oh yeah?

Since when were ordinary dreams so solid, so three-dimensional? As we rattled through grey, shadowy streets, I gave a jolt with every bump beneath our tyres, smelled worn leather all round me and felt a rush of air from the gap at the top of the driver's side window. If this counted as fast asleep what would waking up be like?

"Cyrus?" said Gran.

"Yes?"

"See what I mean? I knew you were up to it. Americans are *born* drivers. It's a well-known fact."

"Gran, I'm not doing the driving. It's your car . . ."

I broke off. What did it matter? ELF 61 was in charge.

Already, beyond the horizon of roofs and chimney-pots up ahead, I saw the spreading, brightening sunrise.

"Handsome, yes?" Gran smiled.

"Brilliant," I answered.

Or tried to answer. My throat was so dry my voice came out as a croak.

"You all right, Cyrus?" Granny asked.

"Fine," I said.

"Me, too."

She sounded so happy I looked away from the road for a split-second.

That, maybe, was my mistake.

Or maybe it would have happened anyway – ELF 61's sudden swerve to the left.

"Hey!" I squawked. "We're on the pavement!"

"Exactly," said Gran. "I should've done this years ago."

"But this is a closed-off street, Gran. Traffic's not allowed here. Only pedestrians."

"That's what they told me," she nodded. "And like a silly old fool, I believed 'em."

"But we can't go this way!"

"Can't we? Strikes me we're doing it."

"Yes, but –"

But what? Wasn't ELF 61 taking care of us? Judging by the easy, chuntering hum of its engine, everything was perfectly under control.

So I sat back and tried to relax. Why should it bother me when we seemed to skip, on two wheels, through a pair of bollards designed to keep vehicles out? Or hopped, bouncingly, over a long stone tub of flowers meant to block the entrance to a narrow alley?

"Posh, ain't it," sniffed Granny. "All these window-boxes and fancy coach-lamps. It's the same old houses underneath, though. The same old streets, too . . . except they've been turned into a blinkin' maze by a load of cluttery, concrete furniture. No wonder

I was always lost before I could get there."

"Why didn't you use the motorway?" I asked.

I snapped my mouth shut the instant I realised what I'd said.

Too late.

Much, much too late.

There was a gleam in Granny's eye now. "Good thinking, Cyrus," she declared. "I mean, while we're at it, maybe we should go the whole hog . . . reckon you could manage it?"

"The motorway?"

"Why not?" said Gran. "We've come this far. And it'll save us a bit of time, that's for sure."

"But we *can't*!" I howled.

I jerked forward, horrified. But for my seat-belt and the steering-wheel, I'd have flattened my nose on the windscreen. How could a dinky, old jalopy like this cope with three lanes of high-speed travelling? Desperately, with the daft notion I might stall the engine or at least bring us skidding to a halt, I wrenched at the steering-wheel.

It didn't make the slightest difference.

ELF 61 was the boss.

With a squeal of tyres which took us the wrong way out of a one-way street we soared up the motorway approach road like a bird winging out of a tunnel and into the sunshine.

"Yippee!" trilled Granny.

"Yippee," I whispered.

Nor did we play safe once we'd got there. Almost before we knew it we were out of the slow lane, across the middle lane and into the fast lane, shimmying madly through the early morning traffic. Well, that's what I think we did. My eyes were shut so tight, I can only guess at the details.

"You sure you're okay, Cyrus?" Granny asked.

"Wonderful."

"Got a lump in your throat have you?"

I shook my head. Just terror deep in my stomach that was all. Especially now I'd opened my eyes.

Slowly, wheel-by-wheel, we were

overtaking a thundering, hissing, ogre-
like lorry which was itself overtaking
another, just the same, on its far side.
Were we really passing both of them at once?

Beep-beep! Beep-beep!

Like a frog giving orders to a couple
of dragons, ELF 61 swept ahead. In
front of us was a long, sleek Mercedes
driven by a man in a peaked cap. Was

he actually pulling over to let us by? Yes! With a cheery wave as we did so!

"It's incredible," I exclaimed. "Can't he see I'm only a kid?"

"An *American* kid," Granny pointed out. "Slow down, Cyrus. We're nearly there."

Coming up now was the junction
where the motorway forks left towards
the city and right towards the coast.

Also a slip-road leading . . . where exactly? A wasteland, was it? Clearly that's where ELF 61 was taking us.

"Lovely, isn't it?" said Gran as we left the slip-road behind.

Lovely? This place? We scrunched across gravel and a grassy track, then came to a stop.

"Really lovely," Gran said.

It was wild, admittedly. Mud and tall weeds, for the most part,

interrupted here and there by stretches of stinky-looking water. Dotted about were piles of sand and rough stones beside a pyramid of criss-crossed, concrete girders. High above these soared a pair of rusty-looking cranes – much taller than the clump of trees standing against the long curve of the motorway where Granny's eyes were fixed. Were the trees part of a garden once? Or maybe a park? So far only the tips of their topmost branches glittered gold and green-ish in the sun.

"Hey," I said. "I know those trees . . . "

Gran nodded. "You can see them from the backyard of my old house," she said. "Well, just the tops of them. But this is the place for a proper view." She was tugging at something tucked beneath her coat and dressing-gown.

78

Her seat-belt was getting in the way.
"Drat it!" she grumbled. At last she
jerked it loose.

It was the picture of Grandpa Mick.

Granny sighed as she turned the
wooden frame this way and that till she
was sure the angle was correct.

"Right here we were – me and ELF

61," she said. "When the picture was took, I mean. Donkey's years ago, of course. But I remember it as if it were yesterday. Micky's last trip home, it was, before he copped it in Burma. He never even knew he had a daughter on the way. Neither did I at the time. That's always been the hardest part . . . "

Her voice trailed away as she went on staring and remembering. All I did was sit there, not saying a word, as the seconds ticked by and the sunlight inched further and further down the trees.

Eventually, Gran said, "'Course, it's changed a bit."

"Has it?"

"All this development, yes. The photo's more like the real thing than the real thing is now. Still, that's only my opinion. Mustn't stand in the way of progress, Cyrus. You'd realise that coming from a country like yours. Pity, though, the way everything has to change."

"Not everything, Gran."

"No?"

"ELF 61's much the same."

"You're right there, dearie. Been a proper pal to me this old banger has.

Couldn't have made this trip without it, you know."

"I'll say."

"Couldn't have made it without you, come to that. Not with the stairs and suchlike and this brain of mine all fuzzy. So I'm really grateful to you for this last bit of fun, Cyrus. Reckon you can get us back home safely before the rest of the house wakes up? They'll make such a fuss if they find out what we've done."

"I'll try, Gran."

"Good kid."

She sank back in her seat. "Don't forget we travel on the opposite side of the road to you," she reminded me. "Always tricky for Americans, that is."

"Easy-peasy for ELF 61," I told her.

And so it was . . . despite the honking, thickening traffic on the

motorway and the backstreets being in broad daylight now.

But the best moment of all came when we were almost home. A police car was tucked in one of the alleyways while its driver had a quiet smoke. I'll never forget the look on his face as ELF 61 hurtled past him – or his frantic smacking at his trousers when his cigarette fell into his lap.

"Won't he report us?" I asked Gran.

"Not with his trousers on fire," Gran said.

We were still laughing about it as we tiptoed indoors and struggled upstairs, Gran clutching at my arm.

"Cheery-bye, Cyrus," she giggled as I tucked her up in bed again.

"Cheery-bye, Gran," I giggled back.

It was even easy-peasy nipping along the landing to the room I was sharing

with Micky for a bit. Except, that is, for dropping my dufflecoat in a heap as I tried to hook it on the bedroom door. Micky sat up at once, rubbing his eyes.

"Where have you been?" he yawned.

"For a ride in Granny's car," I said.

"Yeah?"

"Yeah."

"Very funny, I don't think. Still blinkin' alive is it?"

I crossed to the window and hitched back the curtain. The street was flooded with Spring sunshine but the only movement down at the kerbside came from Sandy rubbing herself against ELF 61's front bumper. Through the glass, I could almost hear her purring.

"Well, is it?" Micky demanded.

"What?"

"ELF 61 – still alive."

By now my grin stretched from ear to

ear. Who wouldn't grin at a grand old car like that?

"Not any more," I said.

This book
was
donated
by

Jean

Burrow